DRIVEN

Written And Published By

MATTHEW DEAN

First edition. May 24, 2025.

Driven

Matthew Dean

Published by Matthew Dean, 2025.

This is a work of fiction. Similarities to real people, places, or events are entirely coincidental.

DRIVEN

First edition. May 24, 2025.

Copyright © 2025 Matthew Dean.

ISBN: 979-8231400669

Written by Matthew Dean.

Table of Contents

Riding Shotgun
The Mystery of the Dashboard Lights

I remember the first time I saw a car as more than a machine. It wasn't when I learned to drive or got my first set of keys. It was much earlier, when I was too small to reach the door handle and too young to make sense of the world beyond the windows. I was riding shotgun, at least, that's what Dad called it, and I had no idea what it meant. What I did know was that the car, in all its wonderful complexity, was a world I couldn't yet enter.

The dashboard lights were the first thing that caught my attention. There was something about the soft glow of those colored lights that captivated me. Red, green, and amber, flashing in soft pulses, like signals from another world. They didn't make sense. I was too young to know that some were warnings and others were simple indicators, that some might be benign and others urgent. All I saw were lights that made the car feel magical, alive, as if each one had a secret to tell.

I would watch them as the car moved down familiar streets, feeling the rhythm of the road in my bones and the way Dad's hands gripped the steering wheel with a quiet assurance. I sat in the passenger seat, my knees reaching the edge of the seat, with my eyes focused on the dashboard. I never asked what they meant, because, in a way, I knew asking would shatter the mystery. The lights were the domain of the grown-ups, a language I wasn't yet ready to understand.

That didn't stop me from imagining. The red one, which blinked in rhythm with Dad's calm driving, was urgent in my mind, a silent warning. I imagined it was telling him to go faster, to avoid something ahead, like an invisible shadow on the road. Or it was calling him to take a different path, one that would lead to places I hadn't yet seen.

The green light was the most soothing. It was the color of reassurance, the pulse of permission. It gave the road a sense of continuity like the world gave Dad a green light to keep going. I saw it as an affirmation from the universe, a pat on the back for driving well, for guiding us safely along the journey.

It was the amber light that captured my curiosity the most. It didn't blink like the others. It glowed steadily, like a question. I would stare at it, wondering if it was asking something of Dad. Was it asking him to be careful? To slow down? Or was it reminding him that the road, and everything about it, was fleeting? Amber always felt like the car was on the verge of something unknown, something that wasn't quite here yet, but coming soon.

Dad, for his part, never seemed to pay attention to the dashboard like I did. His hands were steady on the wheel, eyes scanning the road ahead, but I noticed how his gaze would sometimes turn to the lights before moving back to the horizon. He never spoke about them, and I never asked. It was part of the rhythm of driving, the silent conversation between him and the car.

On long drives, with the windows rolled down and the wind in my hair, I'd lean against the seat and let my thoughts drift. I wondered if Dad knew I was watching. If he sensed the quiet questions in my eyes. Did he know how fascinated I was by the way the car moved? Was it all second nature to him, or did he, too, feel a strange connection to the lights and sounds that made the car feel like it was breathing with us?

What fascinated me most wasn't the dashboard lights or how Dad drove. It was the way he seemed to control everything around us with a slight shift of his hand. It was as if the world outside the car didn't matter as much as the world inside.

I still think about that feeling sometimes when I drive now. The sensation of being in control, of knowing where to go even if I don't know the path ahead. I still glance at the dashboard lights, searching for their secret meanings. Maybe I'll never understand them. Maybe the mystery is the point.

It is enough to know that they're there, quietly waiting to be noticed, lighting the way.

First Time Behind the Wheel

Dad Lets Me Steer

There's a moment that stays with me, one of those rare instances where time seemed to stretch out and hold its breath. I was ten years old, still small enough that my feet didn't reach the pedals, and I had to grip the steering wheel with both hands to feel in control. It was a moment I didn't quite understand then, but one that's woven into my memory like a fine thread, pulling me back to a place where I first learned what it felt like to drive.

It started on a dusty, unpaved road, the kind that twisted and turned through fields and hills, far enough away from town that the only things that knew we were there were the birds overhead and the occasional rustling of the wind in the tall grass. My world seemed to stretch outward, open, endless and full of promise.

Dad had always been a careful driver, calm and steady, with the road a companion he had known for years. His hands rested on the wheel, but there was something in the way he held it that suggested he had nothing to prove. There was no urgency in his motions, just the subtle precision of someone who knew the rhythm of driving, the push of the gas, the gentle press of the brake. He didn't rush. He didn't hurry. There was a quiet confidence in how he moved through the world, and I couldn't help but admire it.

It was on that road, under the wide open sky, that he first let me touch the wheel.

"You want to try?" he asked.

His voice was calm and filled with pride, or was it amusement at the excitement written all over my face?

"Try? Steer the car? Me?"

A rush of nerves and excitement surged through me.

Dad shifted in his seat, making room for me to slide in beside him. I was tall enough to peek over the dashboard, but my feet still dangled just above the pedals. He adjusted the seat forward so I could reach them comfortably.

The leather of the steering wheel felt warm under my palms. It felt solid like the road beneath us, solid like the world outside, solid like this moment, which, for some reason, felt like it was suspended in time.

The car idled. Dad's hand rested on the passenger seat, giving me the green light to take the wheel. His eyes were calm, but I could feel him watching me.

"Don't worry," he said, his voice like the hum of the engine, steady and reassuring. "Steer the wheel. The car will do the rest."

I took a deep breath, feeling the textured surface beneath my fingers. It wasn't like anything I had felt before. It was powerful. The car, this massive, intimidating thing that I had always watched from the passenger seat, felt like a living thing under my command.

I shifted my focus to the road, the dirt path stretching out before us, the occasional bump sending vibrations through the car. I was concentrating so hard that it felt like my body had become one with the car. Every turn of the wheel sent us in a new direction. Even though Dad was there, his steady hand close to mine, he didn't take control. He let me make small mistakes, correcting me only when necessary. Being in charge was both exhilarating and terrifying. It was like walking along the edge of a cliff knowing if you weren't careful you could fall off.

I remember how the dirt road kicked up little puffs of dust that settled on the car's windshield. The world outside felt quiet and far away. It was just me, Dad, and the car, sharing a moment that was ours alone. The engine purred, like a companion telling me I was doing fine, and the car's movements, so smooth and fluid, made me feel like we were gliding, defying the gravity that had always kept me grounded.

When the time came for me to give the wheel back, it felt like the car had become a part of me. I didn't want to let go, but Dad took back the wheel with the same easy confidence he always had. His eyes met mine, not with the look of a parent teaching a lesson, but with a warmth I hadn't expected.

"You did great," he said.

That was enough. I had touched the wheel, felt the road beneath me, and for that brief time, I had driven. The freedom and control it gave me made the world feel smaller.

For the first time, I understood that driving wasn't about getting from one place to another. It was about shaping your own path, with your hands on the wheel and your heart beating to the rhythm of the road. It would be years before I understood the responsibility that came with it.

Borrowing the Keys
(Without Asking)
A Reckless Joyride

The first time I took the car without asking, I didn't even know what I was after. It wasn't about the car. It was about something bigger. Something that pulled at me from inside my chest, a desire to break free, to feel the weight of the world fall away with every mile. There's a moment in life when you realize the power of choice when you understand that for a few minutes, you can control everything. I didn't know the rules then. I only knew that I wanted to feel what it was like to be in charge of my own story.

It started, as these things often do, with a stolen glance. I'd seen Dad's keys sitting on the kitchen counter, right next to the bowl of fruit where they always were. They were a simple set, with that worn, familiar key ring that I had seen a thousand times. That day, they looked different. They looked like a ticket to somewhere exciting, somewhere far from the life I knew.

I remember the heat of the afternoon sun streaming through the windows. It was quiet in the house. Mom was out shopping, Dad was at work, and the house felt empty.

My eyes kept drifting to the keys. What if I took them? What if I drove, for a little while, enough to feel the freedom of the road? I could handle it, I told myself. I'd been in the passenger seat enough times to know how to steer, how to press the gas, and how to follow the rhythm of the road. This wasn't about driving; it was about pushing against the boundaries that had always defined my life.

I grabbed the keys.

My heart hammered in my chest as I stepped outside, the weight of the keys heavy in my pocket. I could feel the eyes of the world on me, even though I was alone. The driveway stretched out ahead, and the car sat parked under the shade of the oak tree. I took a deep breath, hoping I wouldn't hear the sound of a door opening or the creak of footsteps behind me. Nothing came. The house was still silent.

I slid into the driver's seat and stared at the steering wheel. The familiar smell of leather and dust filled my nose. I wasn't supposed to be here. I was doing something I knew I shouldn't. I was breaking the rules and it felt too easy. Either way, I was already in motion.

The engine rumbled to life beneath me. I could feel the vibrations in my chest. The dashboard lights flickered on, welcoming me into a space I hadn't earned. The sound of the car running was intoxicating, and I couldn't resist pressing the gas a little bit to hear the engine rev.

I wasn't a professional driver, but I didn't care. The road was mine. The open space stretched out ahead of me like a canvas, and I was ready to paint on it with reckless abandon.

The car jerked forward as I shifted into drive, the tires spinning a little too fast on the gravel, throwing up clouds of dust behind me. When I turned the wheel too hard, the car swerved, but I didn't care. I was going, and that was all that mattered. The wind rushed through the open window, the trees blurring into streaks of green and brown, and the world shrank down to the car and me. I laughed loud enough to hear it echo off the distant hills.

The laughter didn't last long. Somewhere in the back of my mind, a voice whispered that this wasn't right, that I was crossing a line I couldn't uncross. Fear replaced the thrill of freedom. What if I wrecked the car? What if someone saw me? What if I got caught?

I glanced at the rearview mirror, half-expecting to see Dad's stern face staring back at me. There was nothing. Just the empty road.

I drove on, my heart in my throat. The speed picked up, and with it, a sense of invincibility. I was more alive, with every turn of the wheel, every breath of air that rushed through the window. I didn't want it to end.

The thrill of my joyride began to fade. I realized I couldn't keep driving forever. The car had started to feel heavier, the weight of my own anxiety creeping up on me. I pulled over, shutting off the engine with a shaky hand. The silence that followed was deafening. The reality of what I had done settled in, and for the first time, I understood the real cost of freedom. It was not in the taking, but in the knowing that there was always something left to lose.

I turned the key and slid the car back into the driveway, my hands still trembling. For a moment, I sat there, staring at the dashboard, wondering if anyone would notice. The keys were back in place by the time Mom came home, and Dad never asked about the ride. I knew, somewhere deep down, he must've known. He had to.

I learned something that stayed with me for years. Freedom is thrilling and once you've tasted it, the road will never look the same again.

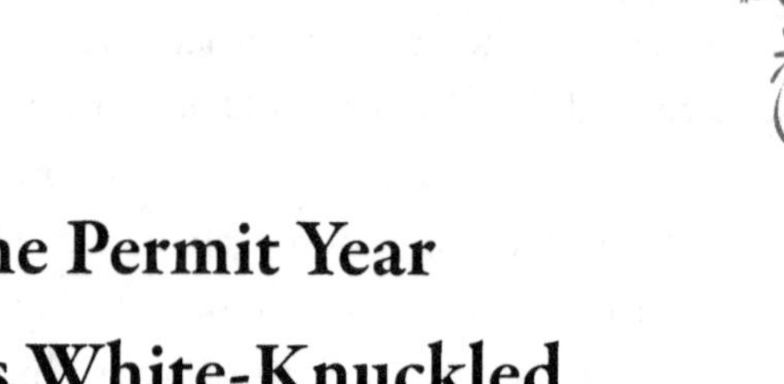

The Permit Year
Mom's White-Knuckled Grip

The first time I drove with my permit, I remember feeling like I had been handed the keys to the kingdom, but the weight of that responsibility didn't sink in until I looked at Mom's face. It was the look in her eyes, and the way her fingers dug into the plastic as if holding on, could somehow protect us both from the chaos of the road.

I wasn't nervous. I had taken online courses, memorized the road signs, and passed the written test. I had mentally mapped out and rehearsed the routes. None of that prepared me for the sensation of driving with Mom in the car. My mother, who had always been in control, now seemed so small beside me. Her eyes shifted between the road and the speedometer, trying to will the car to behave.

We started out on a quiet street, the kind that curved through suburban neighborhoods. The only obstacles were the occasional dog or a neighbor's kid on a bicycle. The morning sunlight filtered through the trees, casting dappled shadows on the road. I shifted into drive, and the car lurched forward.

"Take it slow," Mom said, her voice higher than usual. She was trying to sound calm but couldn't quite manage it. I could hear her hold her breath every time I made a turn.

I nodded, even though I wasn't sure if I was taking it slow. The speedometer seemed to move faster than I wanted it to. I gripped the wheel too tightly, my knuckles pale, but I didn't dare let go. The road was unfamiliar and wide, and I felt like everyone was watching me, judging me.

Mom's knuckles stayed white. Every time I hit the gas, I could feel her shift in the seat, her foot instinctively tapping the floorboard trying to brake for me.

"You're going a little too fast," she said, "and remember, to check your mirrors."

I looked over at her, and she had her eyes fixed on the road, but I could see her hands trembling. She was trying not to show it, but the tension in her face told me everything. Her eyes moved from the road to the side mirror and then back to the windshield like she was taking in every possible escape route in case something went wrong.

I hit the brake, and the car jerked to a stop. Mom flinched. I immediately knew what I had done wrong, and a rush of embarrassment flooded my face.

"It's okay," she said. She wasn't mad, just... scared. I wasn't sure if she was scared of me making another mistake, or scared of the other drivers who never seemed to notice the new driver beside them.

I turned to look at her. Her face was drawn, the lines around her eyes a little deeper than I remembered. She had always been the one giving orders, making decisions, and guiding me through life. For the first time, I was the one in charge, and it made everything feel a little upside down.

I took a deep breath, focused on the road, and when the light turned green, I pressed the gas, letting the car glide forward this time instead of lurching.

"You're doing fine," she said. Her hand relaxed on the handle, but I could still see the small tremors in her fingers. Her eyes stayed on the road like she was willing herself to stay calm for my sake.

I made a right turn into a wider street, and the tires hit the curb. I froze. Mom flinched. She didn't say anything at first.

"Keep your eyes on the road," she finally said. It was a reminder that even though we were both scared, we had to keep going.

We drove for what felt like an eternity, the miles stretching out in front of us, my foot on the gas, my hands gripping the wheel, and Mom's hand loosening from the passenger handle.

The hour passed in fits and starts. There were moments of silence and then moments where I'd check the mirrors and she'd reassure me. By the end of that first drive, I had learned more than the rules of the road. I learned that driving wasn't about controlling the car. It was about controlling the fear that would always be there, whether you were the one holding the wheel or sitting beside someone who was.

That day, I didn't get my first taste of independence. I got a glimpse into the weight on Mom's shoulders. It wasn't about her white-knuckled grip. It was the trust she had to place in me, even though I wasn't ready for it.

Driver's Ed Anxiety
Parallel Parking Panic

The day I learned how to parallel park was the day I realized that no matter how ready I thought I was to drive, the road and the people on it had other plans. I had sat through a hundred hours of classroom lectures about traffic laws, seat belts, and the perils of texting behind the wheel. Each lesson was more monotonous than the last. None of them prepared me for the part where I had to prove I could actually do it. There was no skill more terrifying to me than parallel parking.

The first time I got behind the wheel with the instructor, I had the distinct feeling of being in a pressure cooker. My hands were sweating on the steering wheel, and the air in the car felt suffocating. I tried to remind myself that this was a car and a parking space. How hard could it be? But the instructor's calm, almost robotic voice didn't help.

"Turn right, now left. Reverse. Stop. Turn the wheel."

His voice droned on in that same monotone rhythm that made everything feel like a lecture rather than a lesson. He wasn't mean, just... indifferent. Every instruction felt like a test as if he expected me to fail.

"Do you see the space?" he asked.

I nodded. My stomach churned. I could see it, sure. It was a normal space between two cars, nothing out of the ordinary, except it looked about the size of a shoe box. I tried to focus, but my brain was moving too fast, and my hands weren't catching up.

"Put the car in reverse. Slowly," he said. I felt the car shift, but my foot wasn't gentle enough on the gas, and the car jerked.

"Not too fast."

I looked over at the other cars parked along the curb. They seemed to be watching me, judging me, with their shiny paint and perfect alignment. They weren't about to move. They were waiting for me to mess up, to back into them, to ruin everything. I glanced at the instructor. He wasn't looking at me. He was staring at his clipboard, his pen making slow marks on it with each instruction. It was as if my success or failure meant nothing to him.

I took a deep breath and put the car in reverse again, trying to ignore the pulse of panic growing in my chest. The car was big, and the space was small. I could feel my hands grip the wheel tighter, my knuckles turning white. I tried to remember the instructions. Turn the wheel this way, then that. Back in. My head was swimming with everything I had to do all at once, foot on the brake, hands on the wheel, eyes scanning the mirrors. None of it was coming together. I was thinking too much.

"You're too far over," the instructor said, his voice still detached. "Straighten out."

I looked in the mirror, trying to correct the angle. My heart was racing now, and I wasn't sure if I could keep my hands steady enough to fix it. The car drifted toward the curb, making the whole thing an endless, unspooling nightmare.

The other students in the car, who had already taken their turn, sat silently in the back seat. I couldn't tell if they were watching me or staring out the windows. It didn't matter. The silence made everything worse. It felt like the whole world was holding its breath, waiting for me to screw up, waiting for me to be the one to embarrass myself.

"Pull forward a little, and try again," the instructor said, glancing up from his clipboard. His gaze wasn't even stern. It was matter-of-fact. I wanted to scream. I wanted to pound the steering wheel and demand why this was so hard. I knew how to park. I'd parked in parking lots before, in spaces the same size as this one. This was different.

Would I be the first one to fail? Would this be the moment I'd remember forever? I shifted into drive, rolling the car forward and then back again. This time, I took it slow. I concentrated so hard on my mirrors and the space between the cars that everything else disappeared.

The car inched back with a grace I hadn't expected. I could feel the car slipping into the space where it belonged.

"There. Now straighten it up," the instructor said, a hint of approval in his voice.

I did, and for a moment, the car stood still. I had done it. The tight space between the two cars didn't seem so intimidating anymore. It was a space, a place in the world I could fit into if I concentrated hard enough.

As I shifted the car into park and looked at the instructor, I realized something important. The worst part wasn't the parking. It was the pressure and the constant fear of failure.

The instructor looked up as he scribbled something on his clipboard. "Not bad," he muttered, his voice still flat. It wasn't a compliment. It wasn't even a criticism. It was a statement.

That was exactly what I needed to hear.

Getting My License
Failing the First Time, Acing it the Second

I remember standing in front of the DMV. The knot in my stomach felt like lead. It was the day of my driver's license test, and I thought I was ready. I'd practiced for weeks, driven every route I could think of, gone over every detail, stop signs, parallel parking, and merging onto the highway. I still couldn't shake the feeling that I was on the brink of disaster.

The waiting room at the DMV felt like the place where time went to die. People were filling out forms, and flipping through old magazines, and the clock on the wall ticked away each second. Mom was sitting next to me, her hands folded in her lap, her eyes not quite meeting mine. We hadn't spoken since we left the house. This was the moment that would prove everything. I needed to pass.

When my name was called, I jumped up. The nervous energy in my legs made them feel like rubber. The instructor, a middle-aged man with a tired face and a badge, led me outside to the car. His demeanor was flat and impassive. He handed me the keys without a word, and I slid into the driver's seat, my hands clammy against the wheel.

I started the car. The engine hummed beneath me. The instructor gave me a quick look and then turned his eyes forward, scribbling on his clipboard.

"Drive to the end of the block and turn left," he said.

His voice was as dry as the desert. No warmth. No encouragement. Just instructions.

I could feel Mom's eyes on me from the sidewalk as I drove away. It didn't make me feel better. Instead, it reminded me that there was someone else watching, someone else judging.

The test felt endless. Every turn was a reminder that one mistake could cost me everything. I handled the first few minutes decently. I remembered to signal. I took my turns wide enough so I didn't scrape the curb. Then I made a small misstep. I pulled out of a side street without checking my mirrors. I didn't see the other car coming at the intersection.

It was nothing major. No one honked. No one swerved. I felt it in the pit of my stomach. The instructor's eyes darted to the side. Then he marked something down on his clipboard. I knew, right then, I had already failed.

We drove around for what felt like hours, my confidence leaking out of me with every turn. There was nothing I could do to erase the mistake. I could feel the weight of the test pressing down on me. I tried to focus, to get everything right, but all I could think about was that first mistake. It hung over me like a shadow.

We arrived back at the DMV. The instructor told me to park, and I did, terribly. The wheels bumped over the curb. I had to adjust twice before I could make the car sit straight. I looked at him, but his eyes were already on the clipboard. He nodded toward the curb and muttered, "That'll be all."

I turned off the engine and got out of the car; my shoulders slumped. I didn't need to hear the verdict. I could feel it in my bones. I had failed.

Mom was already there, waiting by the door, her face hopeful until she saw me walking toward her with my head down. The look on her face broke something in me. I had let her down.

"I'm sorry," I muttered as we left the building. When we got to the car, she finally spoke.

"You'll get it next time. Everyone fails once. It's a step. We'll try again."

I wasn't sure if I believed her, but I appreciated the effort. The second attempt felt like an impossible mountain to climb. The next few weeks were spent on the road again. Back in the driver's seat, I rehearsed every turn, every stop sign. I went over the routes and practiced parking in empty lots. I started to feel the rhythms of the car again, the flow of the road, the muscle memory.

This time, I was calmer. Maybe I was more resigned, or maybe I had finally accepted that failure wasn't the end of the world. It was a moment of self-awareness, of understanding that getting things wrong didn't make me any less capable. As we pulled up to the DMV, I didn't feel the crushing pressure I had the first time. Instead, I felt ready.

When my name was called, I didn't fidget. I walked to the car with my head held high. I started the engine, confident and free from the shadow of the previous failure.

The test went smoother than I expected. Every turn was fluid, and every lane change was deliberate. I checked my mirrors, double-checked my blind spots, and didn't let anything distract me. I even nailed the parallel parking, sliding the car between two cones without a second thought.

By the time we were back at the DMV, I felt confident, almost cocky. The instructor didn't offer much feedback, only a nod as I parked the car, but I knew. I could see it in his eyes before he handed me the slip of paper.

"You're good to go."

I got out of the car and made my way to Mom, who was waiting by the door. I could see the smile forming on her face. Seeing the pride in her eyes, I felt all the pressure of the past few weeks melt away.

"Well?" she asked.

I held up the slip.

"I told you," she said, pulling me into a hug. "I told you you'd get it."

My First Car
A Hand-Me-Down Rust Bucket

It was Dad's first, then Mom's for a few years. After that, it sat in the driveway, forgotten. It was parked under a tree, collecting pollen, bird droppings, and layers of pine needles. Over time, it started to look like some ancient fossil from the early days of combustion engines.

I even joked about it: "That thing still runs?" It wasn't much to look at. A lime green 1972 Toyota Corolla with a rusted rear bumper and a driver-side window that didn't roll down unless you coaxed it. The fabric on the ceiling drooped like tired eyelids, the air vents coughed more than they blew, and every time the key was turned, the engine took a second to decide whether it was going to cooperate.

When Dad handed me the keys with a shrug and said, "It'll get you from A to B," I didn't laugh. I stood there, holding the key like it was something sacred.

That first day, I cleaned it out, preparing it for a cross-country trek around the neighborhood. I vacuumed the crumbs and wiped down the sticky residue in the cup holder. I threw out some old water bottles and empty gum packs. I even found a tape of early rock hits jammed under the passenger seat and popped it into the dusty stereo. The speakers crackled, but it worked.

The Corolla didn't smell like a new car. It smelled of old upholstery and engine grease, with a faint trace of Dad's aftershave that had soaked into the steering wheel over the years. When I turned the key and heard the engine come alive, I understood what it meant to be free.

This was my space now. My world with doors and wheels and an ashtray I'd never use but wouldn't dream of removing.

The first solo drive was to the gas station. Five minutes there, five minutes back. I had the windows down, music blaring through the tinny speakers, and I was smiling from ear to ear. Other cars passed me, sleek, polished, whisper-quiet, but none of them felt as alive as mine did.

It rattled over potholes and pulled to the right when I braked too hard. The A/C only worked if I kicked under the dash. That car was the first thing in my life that made me feel big. Not tall or strong, but capable.

Every dent and stain in that car told a story I didn't know. There was a scrape on the back bumper from Dad misjudging the garage and a coffee ring on the console from Mom's early commutes. But the blank spaces, the empty glove compartment, the backseat untouched, those stories were mine to fill.

I drove it to school, to work, to nowhere in particular. I took the long way home because I could. Friends would joke about the missing hubcap and the rattle in the engine, but none of that mattered. When we climbed in, we knew: this was a real car. No GPS, no screens, no sensors to beep when you get too close to a trash can. Just pedals, a steering wheel, and a stereo that skipped on every speed bump. A car you had to feel your way into.

That quiet thrill when you pull away from the curb and nobody's telling you where to go or how fast to get there, stayed with me.

Eventually, the car broke down for good. The repairs started costing more than it was worth, and I had to let it go. That old rust bucket meant the world to me. It was a rite of passage, a battered, faithful companion that saw me through late-night drives, early morning shifts, first kisses, and almost-accidents.

That car never caught anyone's eye. When I was behind the wheel, though, it felt like the road knew my name. I still think about it sometimes. It made me feel like I could go anywhere, and be anyone.

Midnight Roads
Fast Food, Freedom, Cruising with Friends

The road didn't have a destination. That was the whole point.

It was a Friday night, or maybe a Tuesday, or maybe it didn't matter. Time blurred on nights like that, when the only thing guiding us was the streetlight's glow and the sound of the stereo. The car was packed, its suspension more forgiving than it should have been, four bodies crammed in with knees against the dash, shoes up on the back of the seats, and a smell that was equal parts fries, sweat, and spilled soda.

The windows were down, even though it was too cold. The air slapped our faces with the kind of aliveness that only exists when you're seventeen, and the world hasn't said "no" to you yet.

Music thumping through the speakers was loud and distorted, but we sang anyway. Someone was drumming on the dashboard. Someone else was shouting about where to go next. I kept one hand on the wheel and the other draped out the window, pretending I was cool, even though I was hyper-aware of every breath, every turn, every flicker of the dashboard lights.

We never went anywhere. Taco Bell. A gas station parking lot. The dark edge of a park where no one bothered us. The goal was never the place, it was the movement, the inertia, the shared conspiracy of going somewhere else, anywhere, as long as it wasn't home.

Home meant lights out. Chores. Questions. Silence. Out there on the midnight roads, in that box of rusty metal and cracked plastic, we made a home with motion and music and the shared knowledge that nothing mattered except that moment.

Sometimes we'd stop and climb onto the hood, warm from the engine, eating fries from greasy bags and passing sodas back and forth like communion. Conversations drifted from nonsense to confessions and back again. Someone talked about college. Someone else talked about their parents splitting up. Someone, maybe me, talked about feeling invisible at school. I wondered what it would be like to leave this town behind and never look back.

The car made it all possible. It was a mobile sanctuary. A confessional booth. A place to be loud without being told to quiet down. A place to be quiet without having to explain.

There was a night we raced the train, laughing, hearts pounding, the red lights of the crossing blinking as we beat the rumble of steel. There was another night when we pulled over on a back road, killed the engine, and stared at the stars. We talked about nothing for hours. It meant everything.

Every road felt like ours. Even the ones with potholes deep enough to pop the glove box open. Even the ones that dead-ended at cul-de-sacs or stopped cold at construction barriers. We didn't care. We'd turn around, crank up the music, and someone would yell, "Let's find another way."

We always did.

Sometimes, the laughter would fade, and someone would fall asleep in the back seat, slumped against the window, mouth open. The rest of us would get quiet, too, a shared hush settling in as the night got later. I'd drive slower and let the tires and the engine do the talking.

The roads were emptier by then. Occasionally, headlights appeared like ghosts in the rearview. I'd check the mirror, glance at the dash, listen to the rhythm of breathing around me, and feel this strange, aching joy I didn't know how to name.

It wasn't about growing up or breaking the rules. It was about motion. About proving to ourselves that we could go. That we were going somewhere, even if it was around the same old streets.

We were too young to know what we were running from. Or toward. We had the car, we had each other and we had the night.

First Fender Bender
The Awful Crunch Sound

It didn't happen at night, in the rain, or during some high-speed escape like in the movies. It happened in broad daylight, in a grocery store parking lot, doing the most ordinary thing in the world, pulling out of a parking space.

The lot wasn't even full. I had backed out a thousand times before. I wasn't rushing. I wasn't even distracted. I looked. I swear I looked.

But I didn't see.

The crunch was subtle, like a soda can under the tire. A soft, terrible sound, followed by a shift in the frame of the car like something had clicked wrong inside its bones. Time didn't slow down like they say it does in disasters. It stopped.

I froze. Then I turned off the engine.

My first thought wasn't, Am I okay? or Is anyone hurt? It was, How much trouble am I in?

There it was: a low, wide dent across the corner of the bumper. The other car, newer, silver, and spotless, had a matching mark. It wasn't catastrophic, but it was enough to sting.

I stood frozen, wishing the scene would undo itself.

She stepped out of her car. Mid-30s, sunglasses, sharp. She didn't rush. She stood there with a quiet kind of authority. She looked at the damage first, her eyes scanning the dent, then turned to me. There was no panic, no anger.

"You didn't see me?" she asked, not yelling, not mad, just steady in a way that made it even harder to take, as if I had failed some basic test of being alive.

"I—I thought it was clear."

We exchanged insurance info like strangers on a sad blind date. She took pictures with her phone. I felt like I was sinking into the pavement with every shutter click. I couldn't shake the feeling that this was all routine for her, and I was the latest in a long line of idiots who didn't look before backing out.

When she left, I dropped back in the driver's seat and stared at the steering wheel. The dent in the rear wasn't catastrophic, but the one inside me was spreading fast. This was my car. My freedom. Now it was marked with proof that I'd messed up.

I didn't call anyone right away. I sat there, letting the sun roast through the windshield. I didn't cry. I didn't scream. I felt smaller, my hold on a piece of the world I thought I'd earned was gone.

Later that night, I told my parents. I expected the worst. All I got was a sigh.

"Well," Dad said, glancing at the paperwork I'd filled out like it was another form in a long stack of life's mistakes. "It happens."

That was it. It happens.

I expected more than the kind of quiet that says it's time to move on.

The next day, I went outside and ran my fingers over the dent. It wasn't metal. It was a memory. It was shame. It was the first real crack in the illusion that driving made me invincible.

The car still drove fine. The stereo still worked. When I slid into the driver's seat, I felt a shift. I checked my mirrors more obsessively. I backed out slower. I started seeing things, not looking, but really seeing.

I didn't stop driving. The road still called to me, but the freedom it once held was quieter that day. It wasn't empty space beneath me anymore. It was asking more of me. It was the same road, but somehow, it wasn't.

The dent? I never got it fixed. It stayed, a quiet reminder that growing up wasn't some smooth, straight road. It was more like a parking lot, tight, chaotic, and full of mistakes you didn't see coming until you heard the crunch.

Road Trip Romance
A Spontaneous Trip with a New Love

It started as a joke or half a suggestion, tossed between sips of lukewarm gas station coffee and the kind of flirtation that hangs in the air before you name it out loud.

"We should go," she said, legs tucked up on the passenger seat, flipping through a glove box map that hadn't been relevant since before either of us could drive. "Pick a direction and drive."

I said yes. I don't know why. Maybe it was spring and the sky had that bright, waiting-to-be-summer blue. Maybe I hadn't had a reason to say yes to anything in a long time. Maybe when she looked at me like that, half-smiling, one eyebrow raised, daring me, I wanted to be the kind of person who said yes to beautiful girls with messy hair and wild ideas.

The road rolled in front of us like a ribbon, pulling us into the kind of nowhere that feels like everywhere when you're falling for someone. Every mile marker was a countdown to the next thing we didn't know about each other.

She sang loud and off-key. I told stories I'd never told anyone. We played twenty questions and didn't keep score. She reached over and rested her hand on mine like it was the most natural thing in the world.

We didn't have a plan. That was the plan. We followed signs with interesting names, exited for towns we'd never heard of, and made wrong turns on purpose. Somewhere past a county line, we found a diner with cracked red vinyl booths and milkshakes that tasted like childhood. She took a photo of me with whipped cream on my nose, and I let her.

We got lost for real that night. The GPS glitched, and the two-lane road turned into gravel, then dirt. Trees leaned in like they were eavesdropping. I slowed the car, my fingers tight on the wheel.

She didn't panic. She laughed. Rolled down the window and stuck her head out, eyes closed, hair whipping across her face like she was daring the dark to touch her. "We'll figure it out," she said. "We've got time."

Eventually, the road found itself again, and so did we.

We stopped at a cheap motel with a buzzing sign that lit the gravel lot. The room smelled like soap and summer camp. The sheets were stiff. The bathroom fan roared like a plane engine. We didn't care.

We lay on the bed, shoes kicked off, fingers interlaced, talking about everything and nothing. She told me about her first heartbreak. I told her about mine. We shared the same silence after with a quiet understanding that filled the room.

I don't remember when we fell asleep. We woke up tangled together, sun leaking through the curtains, the car waiting outside like it had known all along.

On the way back, we didn't talk as much. Not because there was nothing left to say, but because the silence between us had changed. It was softer now. Comfortable. We didn't need to chase every moment, we were in it.

She leaned her head against the window, feet up on the dash, humming along to a song I didn't know. I looked over at her, and the only thought I had was: This is it. This is what songs are about. Not fireworks. Not forever. A warm car, a full heart, and someone beside you who makes the world feel new.

The road ended. Real life crept in like it always does. For those few days, we traveled on a different map. One that didn't need coordinates.

Only courage, curiosity, and the kind of connection you only find when the destination doesn't matter.

The smiles faded and the love didn't last, but every time I hit the open road, I remember what it felt like to drive to nowhere.

The DUI Close Call
A Near Miss That
Reshapes My Attitude

It was one of those nights that started with warm air, open windows, and the music low. We were out, blowing off steam. I wasn't planning to get drunk. I wasn't planning anything. That's the danger in it, I guess. You don't plan to lose control. It slips out of your hands when you're not paying attention.

A bar. A birthday. A few beers. Enough to blur the edges. Not enough to slur. I wasn't stumbling. I wasn't loud. I was fine. That was the story I kept telling myself.

When we left, someone asked, "You good to drive?" and I laughed. "Yeah, I'm good. I'm fine."

The keys were already in my hand.

I don't remember the drive in detail. That's the part that scares me now. The specifics are gone. Fragments remain: street lights stretching like lasers, the radio playing something with too much bass, someone in the passenger seat scrolling through their phone like nothing was wrong.

The roads were empty. It was late, and everything felt like it was underwater. My hands were steady on the wheel, but I was floating, watching myself drive, trusting muscle memory more than judgment. I took turns too fast. I didn't notice speed limits. At one point, I realized I had turned down a street I didn't mean to. Laughed it off. "Guess we're taking the scenic route."

Then came the lights.

Red and blue. In the rearview.

My stomach dropped in a way no rollercoaster ever matched. That cold clarity hit me like a slap across the face. This is it. This is the moment everything changes.

I pulled over, heart hammering, hands shaking. The officer approached the window with his flashlight. I tried to play it cool, polite, alert, sober enough. He asked where we were headed. I mumbled something about taking a friend home. I kept my eyes forward. Kept both hands on the wheel.

He didn't ask me to step out.

He looked at me for a long time. Like he was trying to decide if I was worth the paperwork, stupid, or lucky.

"Take it slow," he said. "And next time, think harder."

That was it. A warning. A brush with the edge. Then I was driving again, but slower. So much slower.

No one in the car said much after that. I dropped them off, one by one, with a quiet nod or a quick "Thanks." No hugs, no jokes.

I finally parked in my driveway and killed the engine. I sat there in the dark for a long time. The silence roared. I was sick from the realization of how close I'd come to losing everything. One swerve. One red light. One wrong decision.

I didn't drink and drive again. Not even one sip.

The truth is, I wasn't fine. I was lucky, and luck has a way of running out.

It didn't take handcuffs, court dates, or blood on the pavement.

It took a flash of red and blue lights to show me how thin the line really was.

How easily freedom turns dangerous. How fast a wheel shifts from a symbol of independence to a weapon.

I still drive at night. Still roll down the windows. Still love the road, but I drive with more care and with a new kind of awareness that lives in my foot, in my hands, and in the rearview mirror.

The road forgave me once. I won't ask it to do so again.

Learning to Drive Stick

Love, Lessons, and a Few Playful Fights

It started with the stall. Right there, in the middle of a four-way stop, my foot slipped off the clutch, the engine coughed once and died. A small but angry horn blared behind us. I panicked and twisted the key again. She groaned beside me like I'd run over a dog.

"Too fast on the clutch," she said, pointing at the floor like I didn't know where my feet were. "And too soft on the gas. They need to move together, not like strangers on a first date."

She had that look, smug, knowing, infuriating. The one that always made me want to throttle her.

Her little blue Honda Civic was her pride and joy. She drove that little blue Honda like it was part of her body, beautiful, smooth, and effortless. The car obeyed her without question.

I, unfortunately, was all jerks and hesitation.

"Let me try again."

She raised an eyebrow, that smug smile still plastered on her face. "Try not to stall in front of a cop this time, hotshot"

I thought learning stick would be a romantic scene from a movie. She would lean in close, guiding my hands, both of us laughing under the sun as the car bucked like a wild horse.

It was more like boot camp. She barked commands, corrected every movement, and gave sound effects to my mistakes: "WOMP" for revving too high, "BLRRP" for a bad shift, and "NOPE" because.

"This car doesn't like hesitation," she said for the tenth time. "You have to commit."

"I am committing!"

"You're second-guessing. There's a difference."

I clenched the wheel. "You know, you're not actually a great teacher."

She rolled her eyes. "You don't like not being good at something."

That one landed. Square in the gut.

She was right. I hated not knowing how to do this. I hated the lurch and the grind of gears and the feeling that the car was judging me. I hated that she could sit there, calm, legs crossed, sipping her iced coffee, while I fought every inch of the transmission like it was personal.

More than anything, I hated how much I wanted to impress her and how badly I was failing.

After a dozen stalls, a few insults, and one moment where I thought I'd broken the transmission (I hadn't), I managed to get it right. Once. First then second, clean as a whistle.

She didn't cheer. She didn't clap. She nodded. "There you go."

I almost smiled. Then I stalled again.

We sat in silence for a moment, both of us breathing harder than we should've been.

"I'm sorry," I said. "I'm frustrated."

She leaned back in her seat, legs up on the dash now. "I know. It's okay. You're not bad. You're trying too hard."

I turned to her. "That makes me feel better."

That got a laugh. Finally.

"Want a break?" she asked. "You're sweating through your shirt."

"Maybe just a lap with you driving."

She nodded, slid out, and we switched seats. I watched her hands, easy on the wheel, her left foot dancing on the clutch, her right steady on the gas. The car moved like a thought. I couldn't tell where she ended and it began.

We circled the lot in silence for a while. She didn't gloat. She didn't say I told you so. She drove, windows down, music playing low. The fight drained out of us. It never was a real fight. It was two people trying to figure out how to move in sync, in a machine that punishes anything less than perfect timing.

That night, I dreamt of the gearshift in my hand, smooth and stubborn. Like her.

I'd get it eventually. Not the stick. How to meet her in motion. How to match the rhythm. How to stop fighting and feel the machine for what it was.

It would take time. And a lot more stalling.

Breakup at a Red Light
When Conversations Stall in Traffic

It didn't happen over dinner, on a dramatic doorstep, or in some parking lot under the weight of a final argument. It happened at a red light. Three lanes wide, the turn signal ticking away the seconds.

We weren't fighting. That was the strangest part. There wasn't any shouting, no last-ditch efforts, no tears. Only traffic, the late afternoon sun bleeding through the windshield, and the smell of old takeout containers in the back seat.

She was looking out the window. Not scrolling her phone. Not speaking. Staring at the world outside, as if she didn't want to be in the car, in the moment, or with me.

I tapped the steering wheel. Tap. Tap. The light stayed red.

"We should talk," she said, still not looking at me.

I knew the words before she said them. The tone of it. Soft, flat. Not cruel. Not kind. Tired.

I nodded. "Yeah. We should."

There it was. Everything that had been sitting between us for weeks, hovering in the stale air between the dashboard and the glove box. Not a crash. Not a collapse. A slow pull, like the tide going out.

She finally turned toward me. "This isn't working anymore."

I don't even remember what I said. Something like, Okay. Or Yeah. Or nothing at all.

The light turned green, but I didn't move.

Cars honked behind us. Someone yelled.

She looked at the light. Then at me. "You have to go."

I pressed the gas. The car lurched forward. We moved on.

But the conversation didn't.

We drove in silence. Past the mall. Past the strip of fast food joints where we used to park and talk for hours. Onto the exit where I'd normally turn toward her apartment, like muscle memory.

The sun was setting in the way it does when the day feels longer than it should.

At the next light, she asked, "Do you want to say anything?"

I did. God, I did. But I didn't know how to say I didn't know what happened. Or I thought we had more time. Or please don't get out of the car yet. I said, "No."

She nodded.

At the corner by the gas station, I pulled over.

"I'll walk from here," she said, unbuckling her seat belt.

"You sure?"

She looked at me one last time. "Yeah. Thanks for the ride."

She got out. Closed the door. No slam. Only the quiet finality of something that used to matter is over.

I watched her walk. No glance back. Her figure getting smaller in the mirror, swallowed by headlights and strangers and the city that kept on moving, like nothing had changed.

I stayed there a while.

Engine running.

The turn signal still ticking.

The car felt too big and too small. The space between us had stretched to fill it and then emptied out completely.

I drove home without the radio on. Only the rhythm of tires on pavement and the faint echo of words we never quite got around to saying.

Even now, years later, every time I'm stuck at a red light, especially in the late-day quiet, with someone beside me not saying much, I remember that silence.

A Major Accident
Broken Glass and Flashing Lights

Thursday was an ordinary day that felt forgettable until it wasn't. It was the type of day you coast through, brain half elsewhere until a single moment splits your life clean down the middle.

I was in an intersection I'd driven through a hundred times. Windows were down. The radio was low. A to-go coffee in the cup holder. I wasn't speeding. I wasn't distracted. I wasn't texting. I wasn't singing. I was driving, moving forward.

The light was green.

That part I remember clearly. The light was green.

And then—

Flash.

Metal.

Sound.

It wasn't like in the movies. No screeching violins. No slow-motion shout. A blur of color, a truck where it shouldn't have been, and the impact.

The world folded.

There's a moment in every accident where time loses its shape. It stretches and crumples like foil. I remember the feeling more than anything. The sickening lurch. The helplessness. The fact that my hands were still on the wheel, but the car no longer belonged to me.

Then: pain.

Not sharp, not screaming, but there. A heavy ache crawling in from all sides.

I opened my eyes and everything was sideways. Airbag dust hung in the air like fog. The driver's side window was gone, jagged teeth where the glass used to be. I could smell something sharp, burnt rubber, engine heat, and panic.

Someone was yelling. Not at me. Just yelling.

Then the lights.

Red. Blue. White. Flashing in waves that didn't make sense at first. Sirens were pushing through the air like drills.

A paramedic's face appeared in the broken window. Kind eyes, calm voice.

"Can you hear me?"

I nodded. Or maybe I didn't. Maybe I thought I did.

I didn't lose consciousness. That's what they said later. I stayed awake through it all, which made it worse. I got to hear the metal being peeled back. I got to feel the stretcher's straps pull across my chest. I got to taste blood in my mouth and wonder whose it was.

The other driver ran the red light. A mistake. An oversight. A misjudgment. That's what the report would say. That's what his insurance would call it. It wasn't malicious. It wasn't intentional.

It was enough.

A cracked rib. Concussion. Six weeks of physical therapy. The car totaled.

But I was alive.

People said I was lucky. Doctors, friends, and coworkers.

"It could've been so much worse."

I nodded, over and over, because they were right. I was lucky.

But I didn't feel lucky.

I felt broken.

Not in the body. In the trust. In the automatic.

Driving had always been second nature. After the accident, it was like my body had forgotten how to believe in forward motion.

The first time I got back behind the wheel, weeks later, my hands shook. I flinched at intersections. My foot hovered over the brake like I was waiting for another crash to come barreling out of nowhere.

I kept driving.

What else can you do?

You inch forward. You relearn. You stare down green lights with caution. You grip the wheel tighter. You pray, or you pretend. You convince yourself that the world will follow its own rules this time.

The fear fades enough to make room for routine again. For errands and music, and the simple, sacred act of going somewhere.

But it changes you.

Every time I hear a siren now, I pause. Every time I see shattered glass in an intersection, I feel it in my ribs. And every time I drive through that same spot, I hold my breath.

Just for a second.

Because that's all it took.

The Minivan Years
Soccer Practice and Snack Wrappers

There's a kind of surrender that happens when you buy a minivan.

It doesn't matter how cool you are or what you drove in high school. None of that stands a chance against the practicality of sliding doors and stain-resistant seats. You don't choose a minivan, it claims you.

Ours was beige. Always a little dusty. A dent in the passenger side door that no one could remember happening. We named it "The Beast," half-affection, half-apology. It had a mysterious rattle, a blinking check engine light, and enough crumbs in the backseat to feed a medium-sized colony.

It carried everything: diaper bags, soccer balls, science fair projects, forgotten lunches, Halloween costumes, birthday balloons, and one broken goldfish bowl. The cup holders were sticky with juice. The third row had stickers fused to the plastic from some long-ago tantrum. The upholstery smelled like fruit snacks and something sour that no one could ever locate.

Weekdays were a blur of pick-ups and drop-offs. Kids clambering in, shouting over each other, someone always needing to pee right now. There was never enough time, never enough room, and always at least one shoe missing. I'd drive with one hand, twist around to referee backseat arguments and pass napkins over my shoulder like a fast-food concierge.

There were moments, between stoplights and school zones, when I'd catch my reflection in the rearview mirror and not recognize the guy staring back. He looked tired, a little soft around the middle, and like he hadn't heard his music in weeks. Which, in fairness, he hadn't.

Instead, sing-alongs, audiobooks, spelling drills, and the same three pop songs on repeat until I knew every word, even the ones I hated.

It wasn't all chaos.

There were quiet drives, too. Late nights after practices, one kid asleep in the back, the other half-awake, mumbling about school or a friend or a weird dream. Those drives felt holy. The road was dark, the cabin hushed, like we were moving through space together, suspended in our own little orbit. Me, the wheel, and these small people becoming themselves.

Once, during a long trip in heavy traffic, tempers flared. I threatened to pull over and leave everyone on the side of the road. My youngest, eyes wide, asked, "Even Mom?"

That cracked the whole car up. Even me.

That was the thing about the minivan. It wasn't glamorous. It wasn't fast. But it held us. Through the years of sleep-deprived mornings, tantrums in the drive-thru, long drives to grandparents' houses, and that one family vacation where everything went wrong. We all got food poisoning somewhere outside Toledo.

That van was our second home.

The kids got bigger. The messes got smaller. The arguments were quieter. The need for a van... less urgent.

One day, I drove it to the dealership and traded it in for something sleeker, smaller, and quieter.

They gave me a decent deal. Said they'd detail it, and clean it up for resale. I nodded, signed the paperwork, and handed over the keys.

Before I left, I opened the side door one last time. The seatbelt was still twisted the way my daughter always left it. A crayon sat under the floor mat. A hair tie rested on the seat.

I shut the door, and for the first time in a long time, I drove away in silence.

Backseat Parent
Teaching My Kid to Drive

The first time I sat in the passenger seat with my son behind the wheel, I understood my mother's white knuckles.

It was a simple stretch of suburban road. No traffic. No rain. No traffic. My stomach was doing the same slow roll it did back when I used to sneak the car out before I had a license. This time, I wasn't about getting caught; it was about letting go.

He adjusted the mirrors, and the seat, and fumbled with the seatbelt even though we'd gone over it a dozen times. I could see his hands trembling. Not a full shake, but that taut, nervous energy, like a guitar string tuned too tight.

"You good?" I asked.

He nodded, trying to look casual. "Yeah. I think so."

When the car jerked forward, I instinctively reached for the dashboard. That parental reflex.

"Sorry."

"It's fine," I lied.

It wasn't fine. It was terrifying. Not because he was bad at it, they weren't. It was terrifying because this was the beginning of something I couldn't control. He was going to make mistakes. He was going to get hurt. Maybe not today. Maybe not behind the wheel. But at some point.

And I wouldn't be able to stop it.

We crawled down the block, every mailbox a threat, every parked car a hazard. I heard my voice come out too sharp when he turned too wide: "Watch it, watch your angle!"

He flinched. "I am watching."

I exhaled. Counted to three. "Okay. Sorry. You're doing fine."

We drove in slow circles around the neighborhood. I watched his eyes check the mirrors, and his hands correct themselves on the wheel. I gave him pointers. Gentle ones, when I remembered how. In the quiet moments, I stared out the window and realized: I'd been here before. Just not in this seat.

I remembered my own first drives. The thrill. The panic. The quiet judgment from Mom beside me. I remembered the first time I took the car out alone. How the silence in the cabin felt like freedom, like trust, like possibility.

Now I was the one handing it over.

After a while, we pulled over. He leaned back in the seat and looked at me.

"That was okay, right?"

I smiled. "It was better than okay."

I got behind the wheel for the drive home. He queued up music on his phone. It was something I didn't know but didn't hate. The sun was setting, washing the streets in that soft amber that makes everything look like a memory before it even ends.

"Thanks."

I glanced over. "For what?"

"For not freaking out too bad."

I laughed. "You did great. And freaking out is part of the job."

He smiled and looked out the window.

We didn't talk much on the way home.

He would be driving on his own soon. Getting his license. Pulling out of the driveway while I stood at the window, pretending not to worry. The way my parents must have done. The way every parent does.

Teaching him to drive wasn't about turn signals and speed limits. It was about letting go and trusting that he would find his own road and his own rhythm. Even if I couldn't be there to tell them when to brake.

My Dream Car
The Car I Always Wanted
and Being Bored By It

It's funny how life works. For years, I dreamed about The Car. The one that existed in my head like a myth, sleek, powerful, mine. I first drove one in my twenties: the engine's roar, the leather seats, the way it would make me feel when I turned the key. That feeling never left me.

It wasn't about the car. It was what the car represented. It was freedom. It was success. It was that moment when I'd arrived. It was my reward, a symbol of all the long nights, the sacrifices, the hard work that had finally paid off.

I walked into the dealership with my checkbook, ready to make history. Stepping through the doors was walking into a dream. There it was. The Car. Waiting. The color was perfect. The trim, the rims, and the bumpers, all gleamed like it was built only for me.

I slid into the seat, my hands finding the wheel. That unmistakable new car smell wrapped around me. I felt that deep, quiet rush you only get when something you've dreamed about finally becomes real.

I drove off the lot with the smile of a lottery winner. The tires whispered against the asphalt, and the engine roared. Every surface, every dial, and every stitch was a quiet reminder that this wasn't a car. It was The Car. The one I'd dreamed of for thirty years. It was everything I'd imagined and more.

For the first few months, I couldn't get enough of it. I drove just to drive. I'd take the long way home. I'd sit in the parking lot after work for no reason other than to enjoy the feel of the car. It became part of my identity. It was something I was proud of, something I'd earned. I posted pictures of it. I showed it off to friends. "Check out the ride," I'd say. There was no mistaking the pride in my voice.

The novelty started to fade. Slowly, almost imperceptibly at first, but it was there. The engine still hummed perfectly. The leather seats were still pristine. But the thrill faded. The drive wasn't quite as exciting anymore. The road felt a little emptier. The car became a tool for getting from one place to another. It was exactly what it was meant to be, but nothing more.

I started noticing little things that annoyed me. The sound of the AC wasn't as smooth as I remembered. The seat was a little too low, and I kept adjusting it. I found myself glancing at my phone more often, zoning out in traffic as if the car didn't demand the attention it once did.

I still had my dream car, but now it just... was. The way it looked, the way it felt, it didn't mean anything anymore. I wasn't the guy in the story having it all. I was a guy with a car.

I still drove it, but it was no longer an escape. No longer a triumph. It had become routine, another thing that fit into my schedule. I didn't take the long way home anymore. I didn't drive for the sake of driving.

I parked it in the driveway. I wiped the dust off the hood. When people came over, I'd still point it out, but the shine was different now. It had dulled. Not the car. It was still in perfect condition. I had changed.

That's the real lesson of the dream car. It's not that you stop wanting it, or that you should stop dreaming. When you get what you've always wanted, you realize it wasn't what you were after. It was the idea of it. The possibility. The belief that something outside of yourself would finally fill that hollow space.

But the space remains.

The Doctor's Warning
A Conversation About Reaction Time

The visit was routine. Or, at least, that's how I thought of it. A check-up, a renewal of prescriptions, and a little chat about diet or exercise. I hadn't expected it to feel like a turning point or a diagnosis.

When Dr. Palmer began talking about reaction times and vision, something inside me stiffened. It wasn't the words themselves; they were clinical, measured, and impersonal. It was the fact that he was talking to me. Talking about things that felt... far away. The kind of things that only happen to other people.

"You're doing well, generally," he said, flipping through my chart, not looking up from the paper. "But as you get older, your reflexes slow down a bit. It's natural, of course. The trick is being aware of it. Reaction time gets a little slower. You'll notice it more when you're driving."

I nodded, distracted. Until he paused and set the chart down.

"Have you considered what kind of car you're driving?"

The question took me by surprise. "What do you mean?"

"Well, your reaction time might be slower now, and that's something you have to take into account. Things like the car's safety features, the ability to stop quickly, and the ease of maneuvering matter more as you get older. Something more forgiving, more responsive. It could help."

I didn't say anything at first. I felt self-conscious. I wasn't doing something wrong. Why was he talking about me, but not to me. The doctor wasn't scolding me; he was stating facts. But the facts felt... heavy. My reflexes weren't what they used to be. My vision wasn't either. The thought hit me like a fist to the gut: I'm not young anymore.

That evening, I found myself at the dealership. I had no real plan, just a feeling that I should go and look around.

The lot was full of sporty sedans and fast coupes. They looked so good, so sleek. When I turned the corner, I saw it. It was an old person's car. That's what my younger self would have called it: a soft burgundy sedan, wide, spacious, with a rounded shape and a trunk that seemed to go on for days. Nothing sleek about it. Nothing exciting. It sat there, parked in the corner of the lot, looking steady, reliable, and safe.

I stood there for a while, the sound of the lot fading into a dull hum. I remember riding in a car like this with my parents in the front seat. They'd been in their fifties then, too young for what I thought of as "old people's cars," but that's exactly how I'd seen them. The kind of cars that represented slowing down, retreating from the world, and making peace with getting older.

Here I was, contemplating one for myself.

I test-drove it the next day.

It wasn't thrilling. There was no roar of the engine, no rush of acceleration. It was smooth. Calm. Predictable. The steering was soft, and the seats were comfortable. It had every safety feature you could imagine, lane assist, automatic braking, and blind spot detection. Features I would have rolled my eyes at once upon a time.

The more I drove it, the more something inside me settled. The seats cradled me, the steering wheel felt right under my fingers, and the car responded with a calm efficiency that The Car could never match.

For the first time in a long time, I didn't feel I was trying to prove anything. I wasn't in a race. I wasn't trying to hold on to something that was slipping away.

I drove back to the dealership and signed the papers. I was trading in my dream car for a car that fit better, a car that acknowledged my age without shame. I wasn't giving up. I was changing lanes.

Keys on the Hook
Surrendering the License

I'd known it was coming for a while.

The first sign was subtle, almost imperceptible, a tiny tremor in my hands when I gripped the wheel. I didn't think much of it at first. I told myself it was nothing. I hadn't slept well, or my grip wasn't as firm as it used to be. It was easy to ignore. I'd been driving for so long, it was a fluke.

The signs kept piling up.

Reaction times were slower when the light turned yellow. The hesitant pauses at the intersection, the split-second uncertainty before making a turn. I found myself adjusting the mirrors more often, squinting at the road, and, worst of all, forgetting what I had intended to do once I reached my destination. It wasn't a single moment of clarity; it was a series of them. It was a creeping awareness that I no longer had the same control I once had.

Then, one day, after pulling over to the side of the road because my head had felt too heavy, my hands too unsteady, I knew. It was time. Time to stop. Time to step aside.

I drove home that day, parked the car in the garage, and sat there for a while, staring at the dashboard, waiting for the car to tell me what to do next. It didn't answer.

The conversation with my kids started in bits and pieces. It wasn't immediate. At first, I brushed it off when they asked. "You're getting older, Dad. Do you think maybe it's time to think about not driving?" They didn't say it, but I could hear the concern in their voices. They could see the same things I was trying to ignore.

"I'm fine," I'd say. "I'm just a little tired today." I could tell they weren't convinced. They'd watch me after every drive, waiting for me to admit what was happening before I knew it myself.

One night, after dinner, my youngest son looked me in the eye and said, "Dad, we're worried. You're not driving safely anymore. I think it's time we take the keys."

His words weren't accusatory. There was no anger or frustration in his voice, only the quiet fear of someone who had watched a loved one drift a little too far down a road they couldn't come back from. That's when I knew he was right. It wasn't my own fear anymore; it was theirs too.

The next morning, I found myself standing at the kitchen counter, the keys to my car in my hand. They felt heavy. I thought about all the times I'd grabbed them without a second thought, me, the road, and the endless horizon.

I walked out to the garage, where they were waiting. My son and daughter stood there, their expressions serious but gentle. There was no judgment in their eyes, just concern. I handed over the keys without a word. They took them with that same quiet respect.

I could have said something. I could have explained. I didn't need to. The moment spoke for itself. I wasn't ready to let go, but I knew this wasn't about me anymore. This was about them.

I sat on the front porch as my son drove the car away for the last time. He drove slowly at first like he wasn't sure how it would feel, either. As the car picked up speed and disappeared down the street, I felt something shift. It wasn't about the car leaving. It was the one thing I had been avoiding. The loss of independence. The understanding that I wouldn't be behind the wheel again.

I watched the taillights fade into the distance and felt an unexpected calm settle over me. The road had gotten too long.

I didn't drive again after that. The garage sat empty, and there were no keys on the hook. I found peace, not in letting go, but in gratitude for every mile I had traveled. Life, like any good road, isn't measured by how far you drive, but by how fully you lived the journey, and mine had been full.

About the Author

Matthew Dean is a writer whose work explores the intersections of memory, identity, and the human experience. Inspired by both personal journeys and universal truths, his stories invite readers into narratives rich with depth and authenticity. He lives in Houston, Texas, where he continues to write and reflect on the paths that shape us.

Don't miss out!

Visit the website below and you can sign up to receive emails whenever Matthew Dean publishes a new book. There's no charge and no obligation.

https://books2read.com/r/B-A-VRFXD-OOAJG

BOOKS 2 READ

Connecting independent readers to independent writers.

About the Author

Matthew Dean is a writer whose work explores the intersections of memory, identity, and the human experience. Inspired by both personal journeys and universal truths, his stories invite readers into narratives rich with depth and authenticity. He lives in Houston, Texas, where he continues to write and reflect on the paths that shape us.

www.ingramcontent.com/pod-product-compliance
Lightning Source LLC
Chambersburg PA
CBHW070555160726
48003CB00005B/2062